Dear Parent:
Your child's love of reading starts here!

Every child learns to read in a different way and at his or her own speed. Some go back and forth between reading levels and read favorite books again and again. Others read through each level in order. You can help your young reader improve and become more confident by encouraging his or her own interests and abilities. From books your child reads with you to the first books he or she reads alone, there are I Can Read Books for every stage of reading:

SHARED READING
Basic language, word repetition, and whimsical illustrations, ideal for sharing with your emergent reader

BEGINNING READING
Short sentences, familiar words, and simple concepts for children eager to read on their own

READING WITH HELP
Engaging stories, longer sentences, and language play for developing readers

READING ALONE
Complex plots, challenging vocabulary, and high-interest topics for the independent reader

ADVANCED READING
Short paragraphs, chapters, and exciting themes for the perfect bridge to chapter books

I Can Read Books have introduced children to the joy of reading since 1957. Featuring award-winning authors and illustrators and a fabulous cast of beloved characters, I Can Read Books set the standard for beginning readers.

A lifetime of discovery begins with the magical words **"I Can Read!"**

Visit www.icanread.com for inforn
on enriching your child's reading ex{

D0180911

MAN OF STEEL™

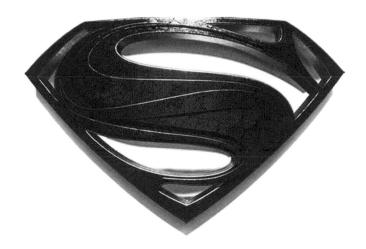

I Can Read Book® is a trademark of HarperCollins Publishers.

Man of Steel: Superman's Superpowers
Copyright © 2013 DC Comics.
SUPERMAN and all related characters and elements are trademarks of and © DC Comics.
(s13)

HARP29824

All rights reserved. Printed in the United States of America. No part of this book may be used or reproduced in any manner whatsoever without written permission except in the case of brief quotations embodied in critical articles and reviews. For information address HarperCollins Children's Books, a division of HarperCollins Publishers, 10 East 53rd Street, New York, NY 10022.
www.icanread.com

Library of Congress catalog card number: 2012955960
ISBN 978-0-06-223597-8

Book design by John Sazaklis

13 14 15 16 17   LP/WOR   10 9 8 7 6 5 4 3 2 1

❖

First Edition

I Can Read!™ Reading 2 With Help

MAN OF STEEL™

Superman's Superpowers

Adapted by Lucy Rosen
Illustrated by Andie Tong
Cover art by Jeremy Roberts

Inspired by the film MAN OF STEEL
Screenplay by DAVID S. GOYER
Story by DAVID S. GOYER and CHRISTOPHER NOLAN
SUPERMAN created by JERRY SIEGEL and JOE SHUSTER

HARPER
An Imprint of HarperCollins*Publishers*

Jonathan and Martha Kent lived

on a farm in Smallville, Kansas.

They had a young son

named Clark.

Their terrier's name was Shelby.

The Kents were a very

loving family.

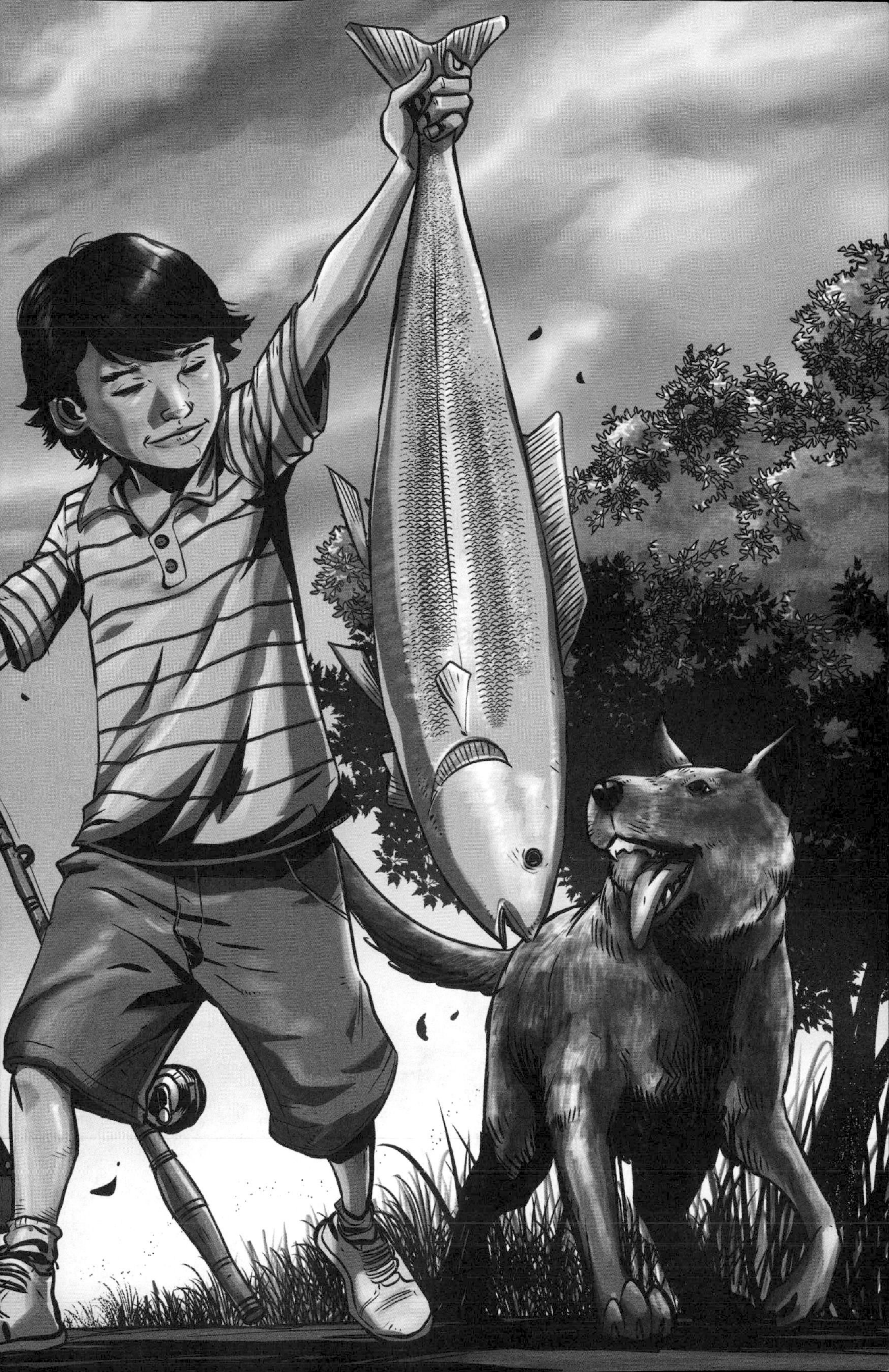

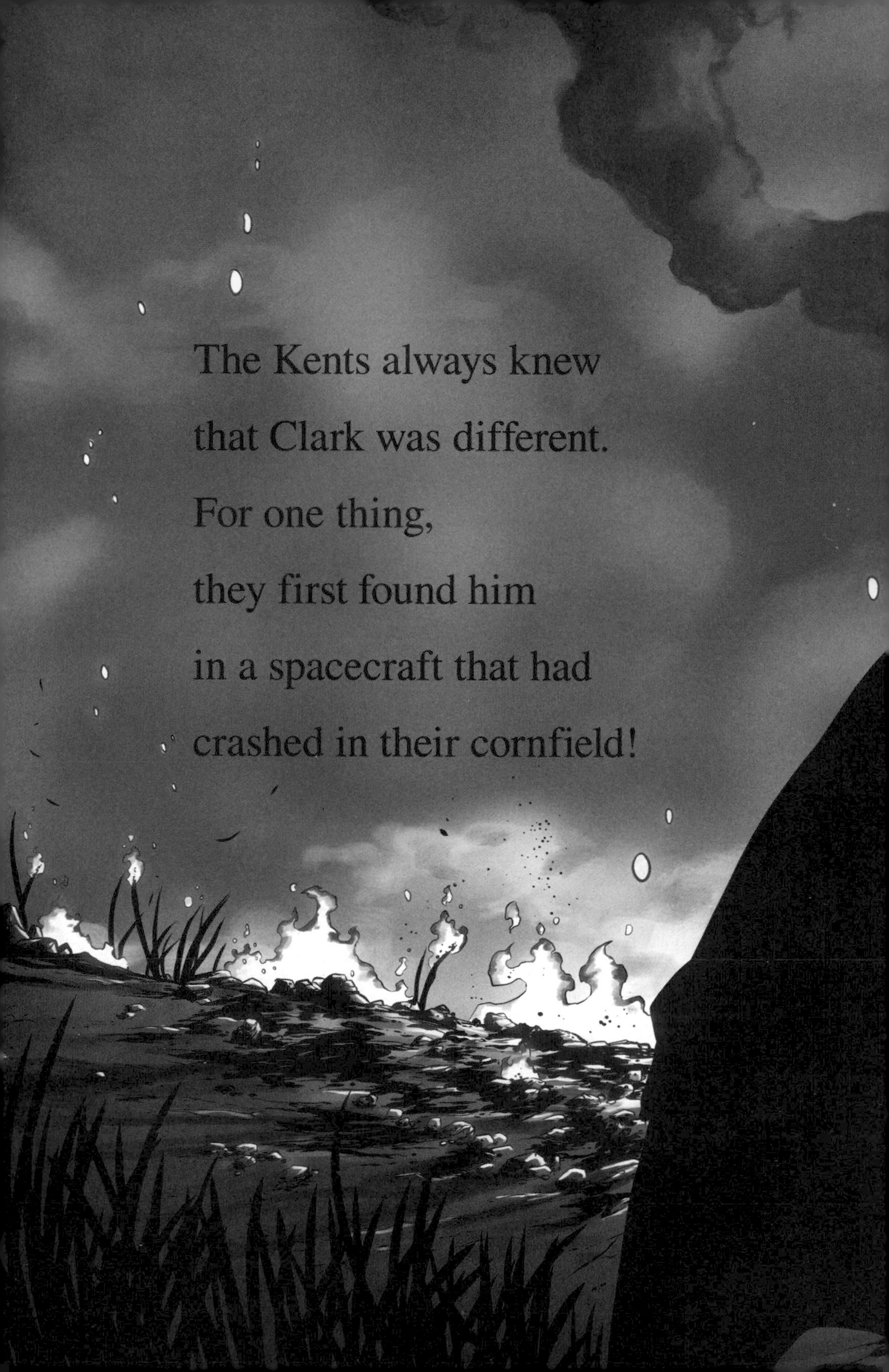

The Kents always knew
that Clark was different.
For one thing,
they first found him
in a spacecraft that had
crashed in their cornfield!

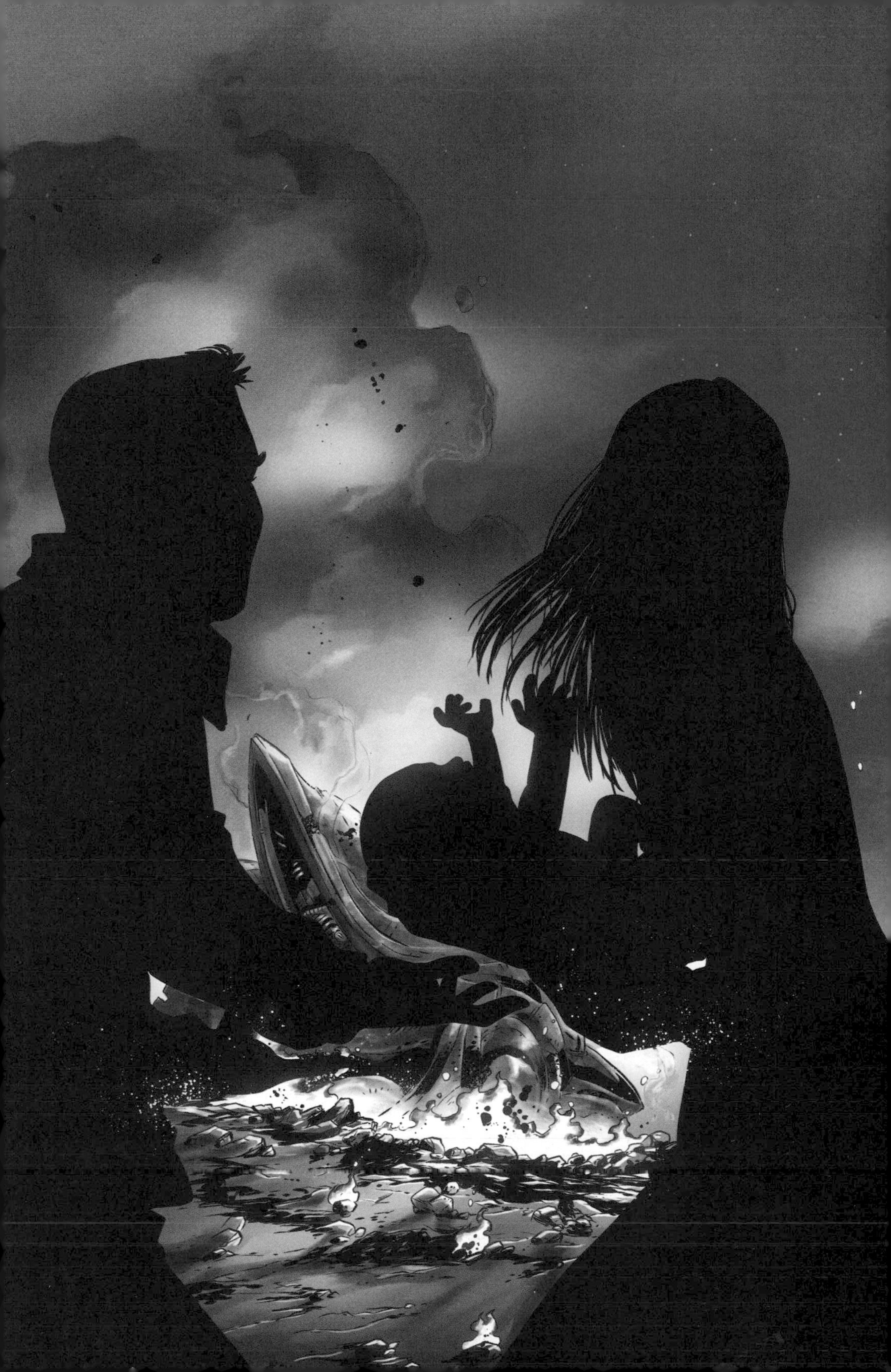

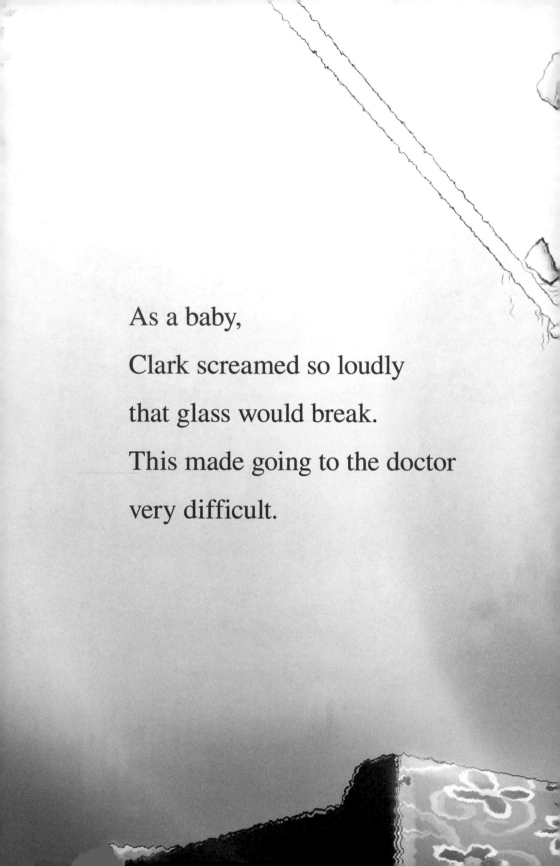

As a baby,

Clark screamed so loudly

that glass would break.

This made going to the doctor

very difficult.

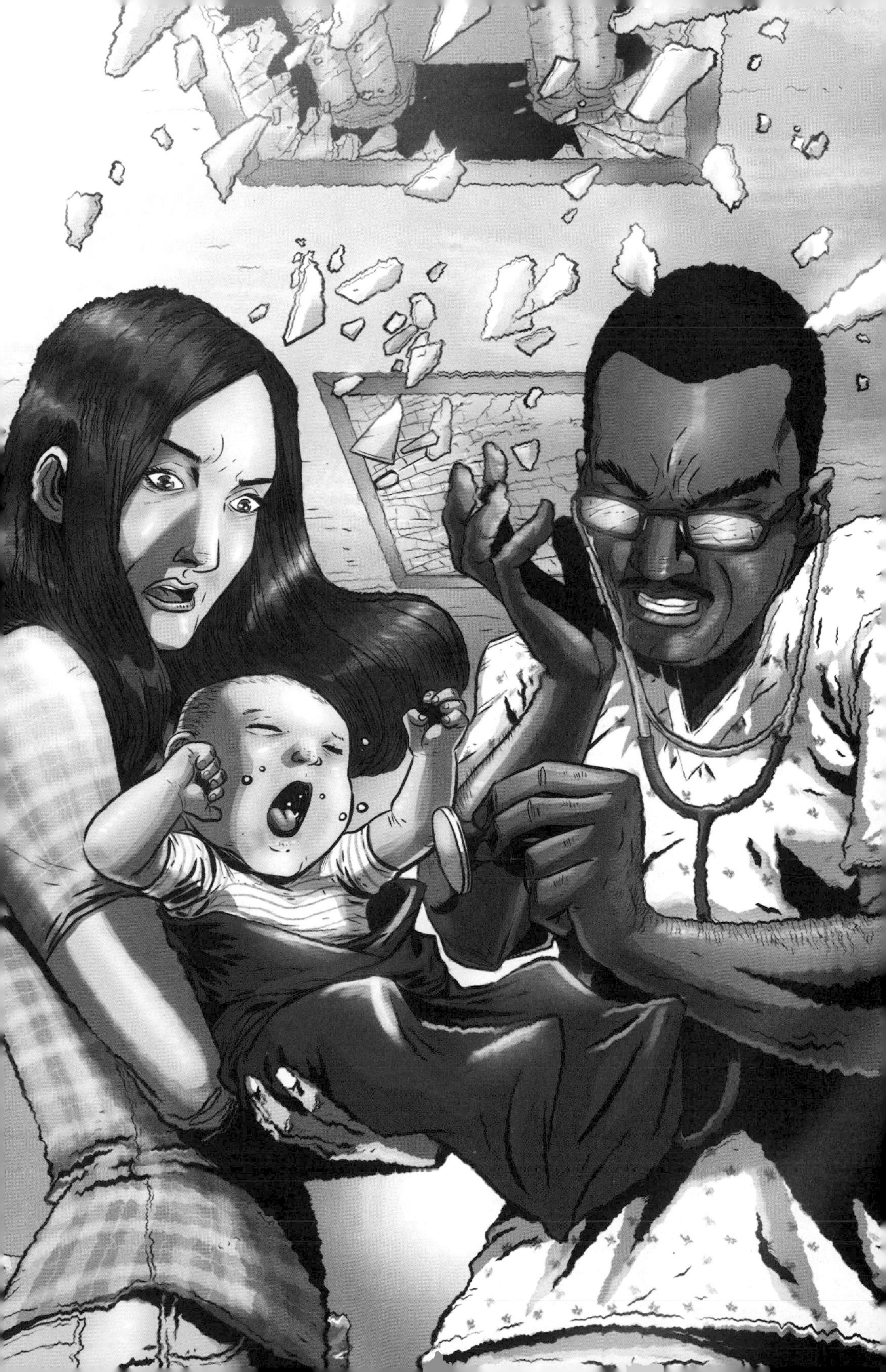

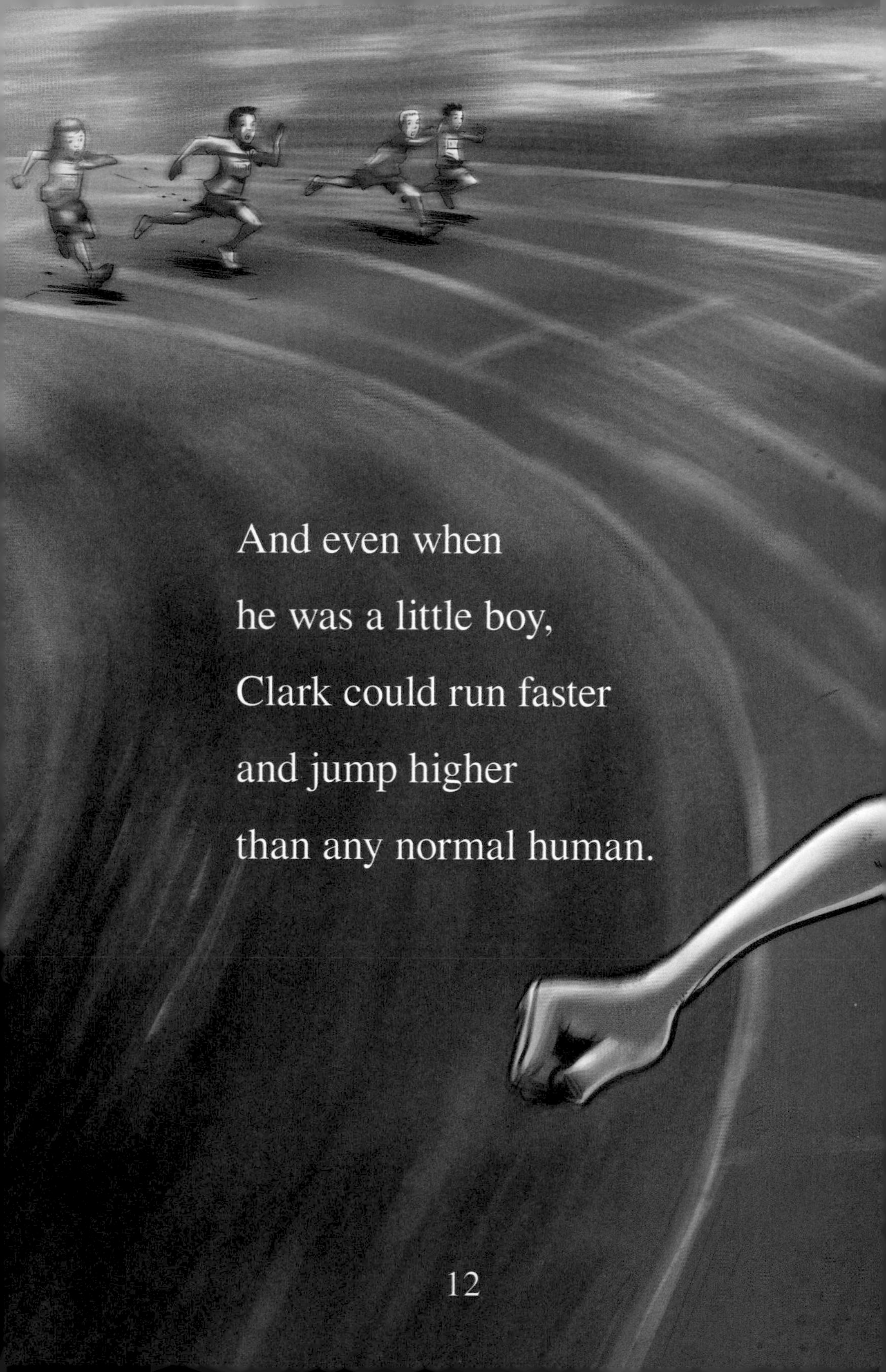

And even when
he was a little boy,
Clark could run faster
and jump higher
than any normal human.

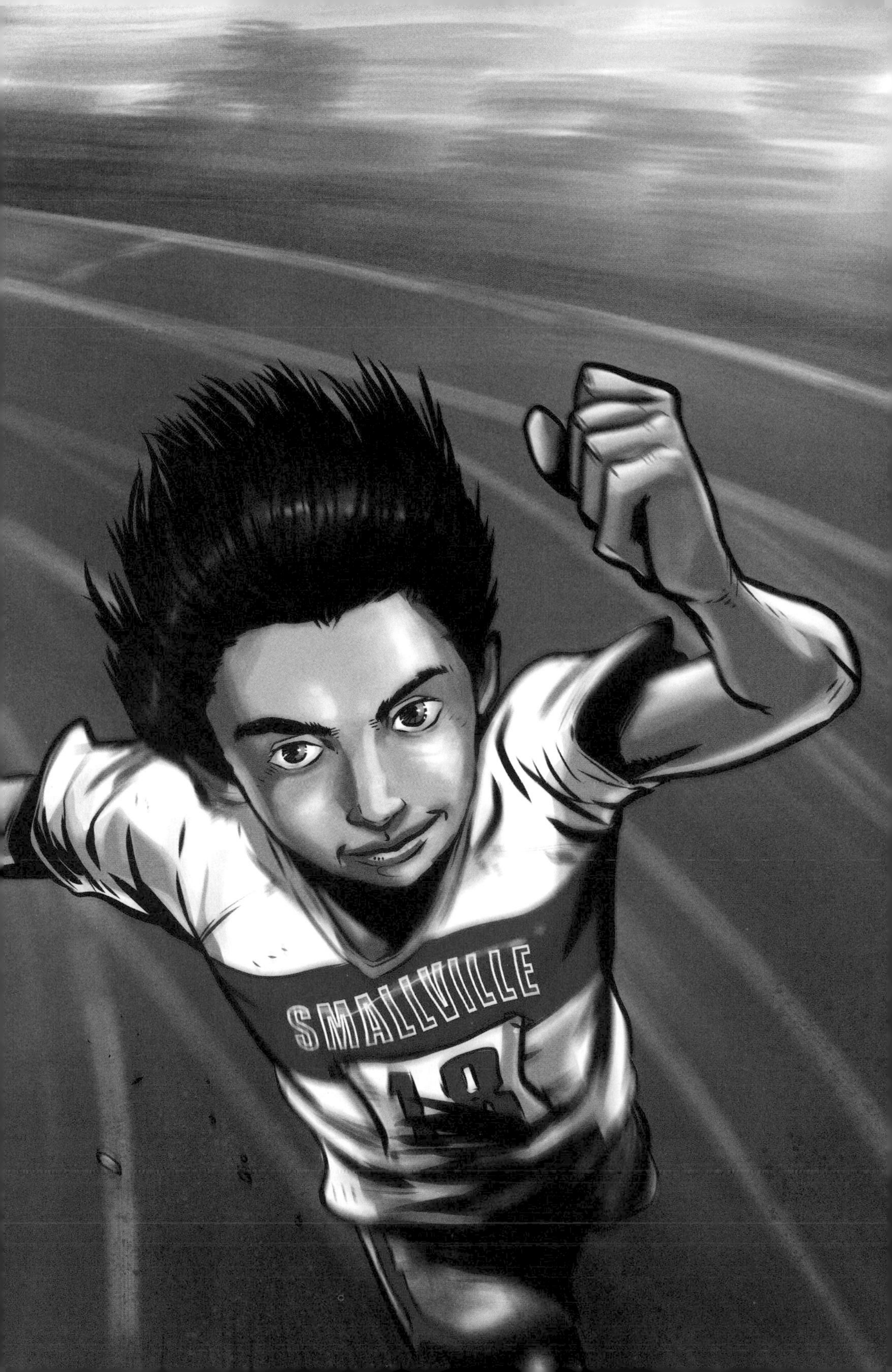
SMALLVILLE

One day on the farm,

Clark closed his eyes for a second.

When he opened them back up,

he couldn't believe what he saw.

Instead of the animals,

Clark saw skeletons all around him!

He had suddenly developed

X-ray vision!

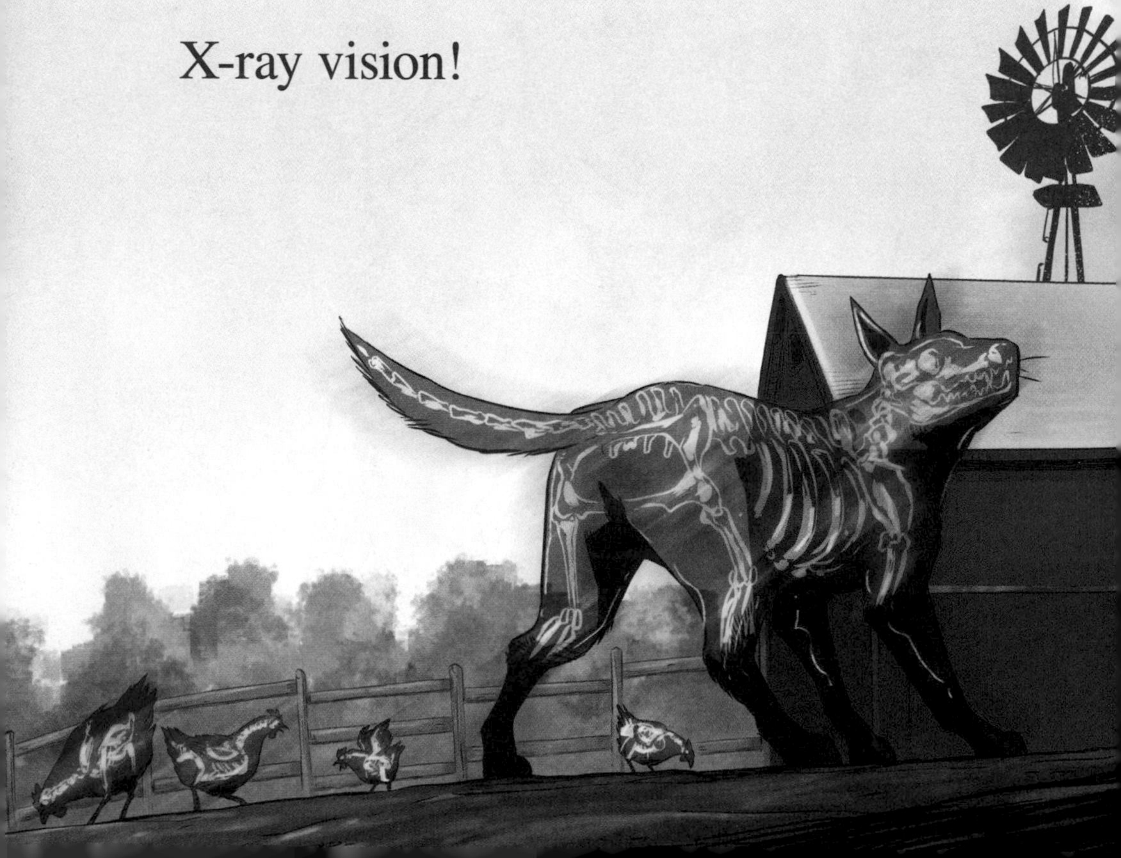

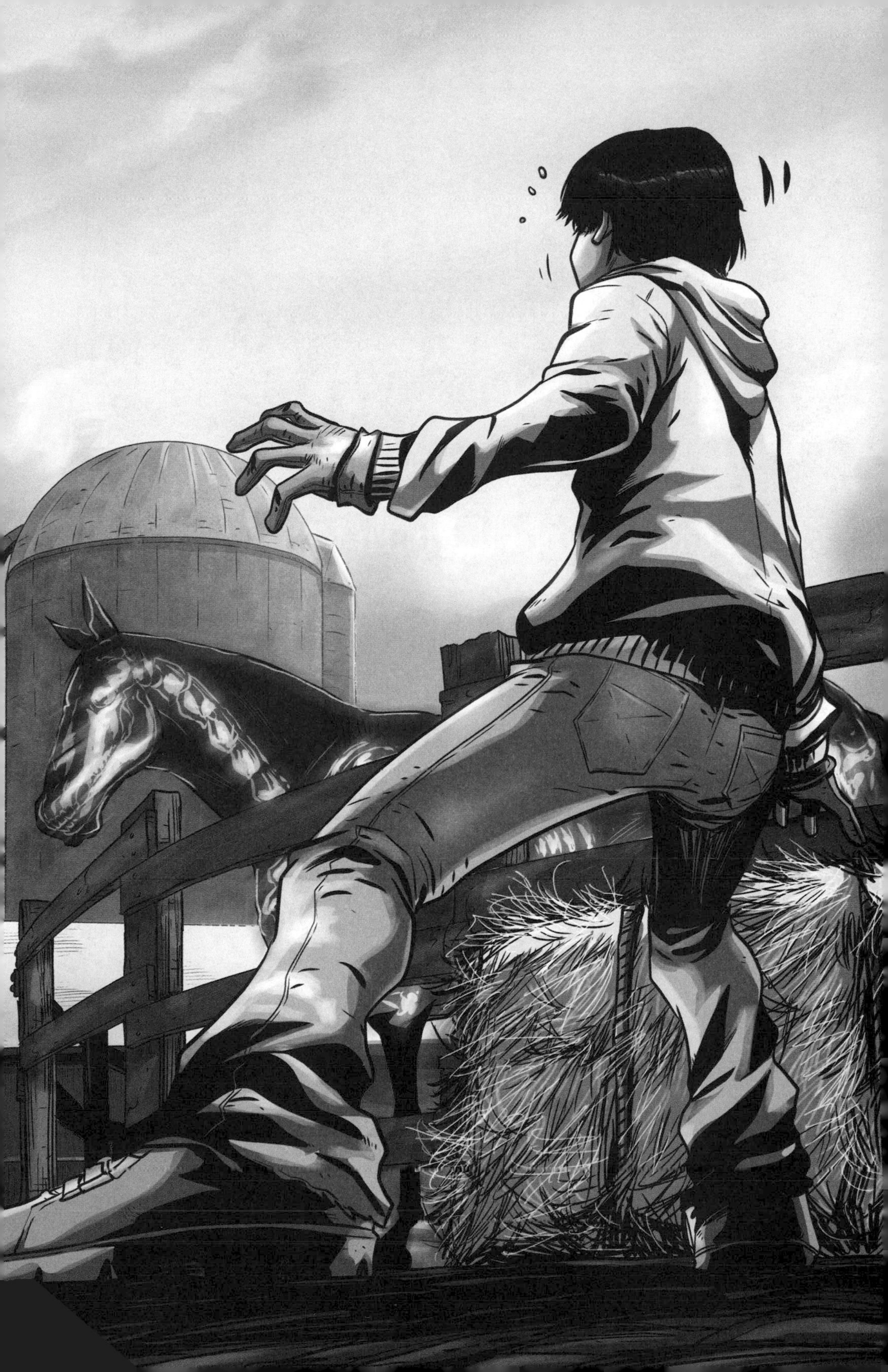

“What’s going on?”
Clark said to himself.
He started getting scared.
Clark ran into the barn to hide.
His eyes began to itch and burn.
Two red-hot laser beams shot out,
setting a hay bale on fire!

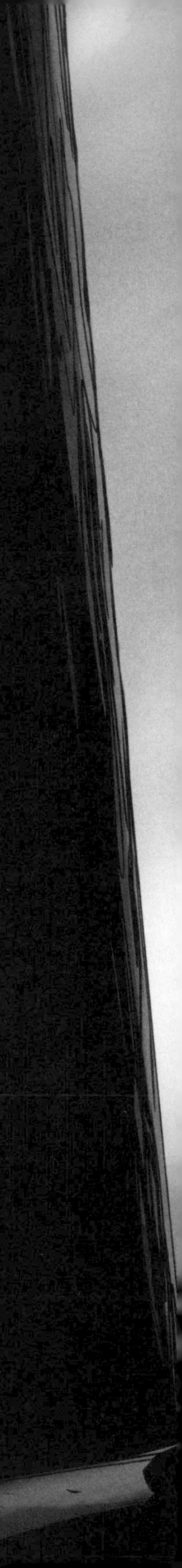

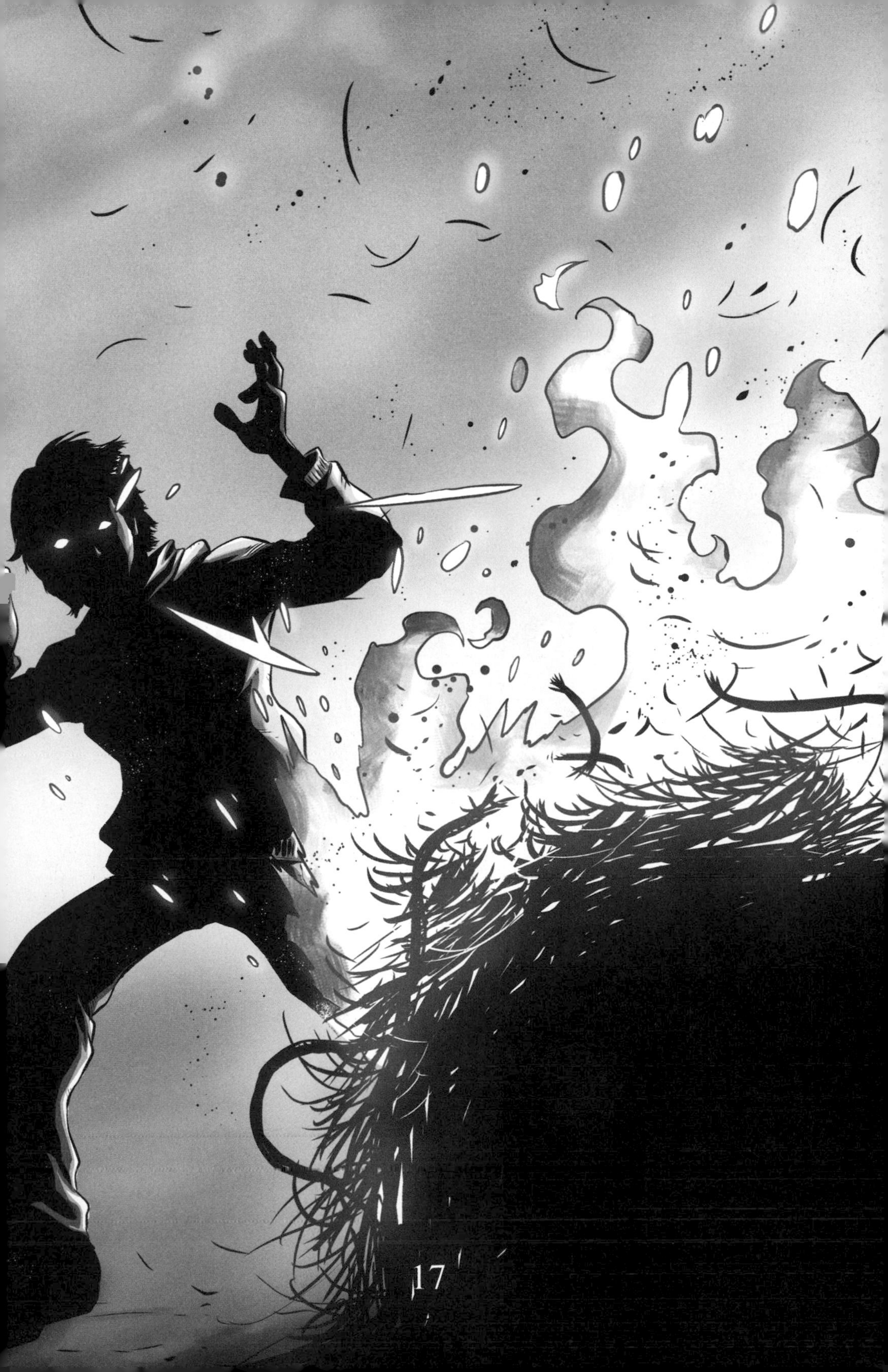

That night,

Clark told his mom and dad

how much his powers scared him.

"You have a choice," his dad said.

"You can run away from who you are,

or you can use your gifts to help others.

Choose who you want to be,

because that person can

change the world, for good or bad."

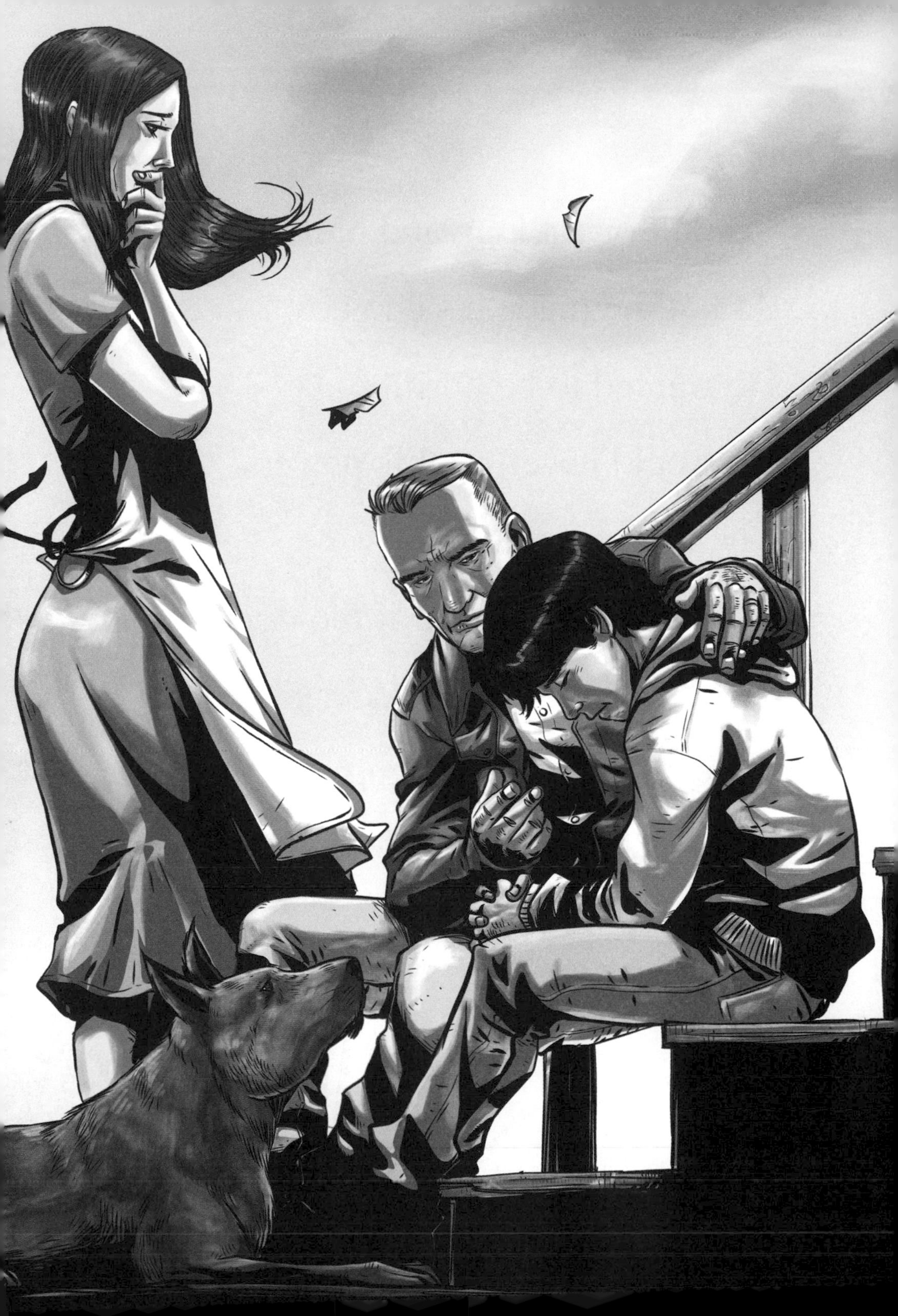

Clark thought long and hard.

At last, he made his choice.

He wanted to be normal.

He would never use his powers.

Then one afternoon,

Jonathan lost control of the tractor.

Their pet, Shelby, darted right into

the path of the oncoming vehicle.

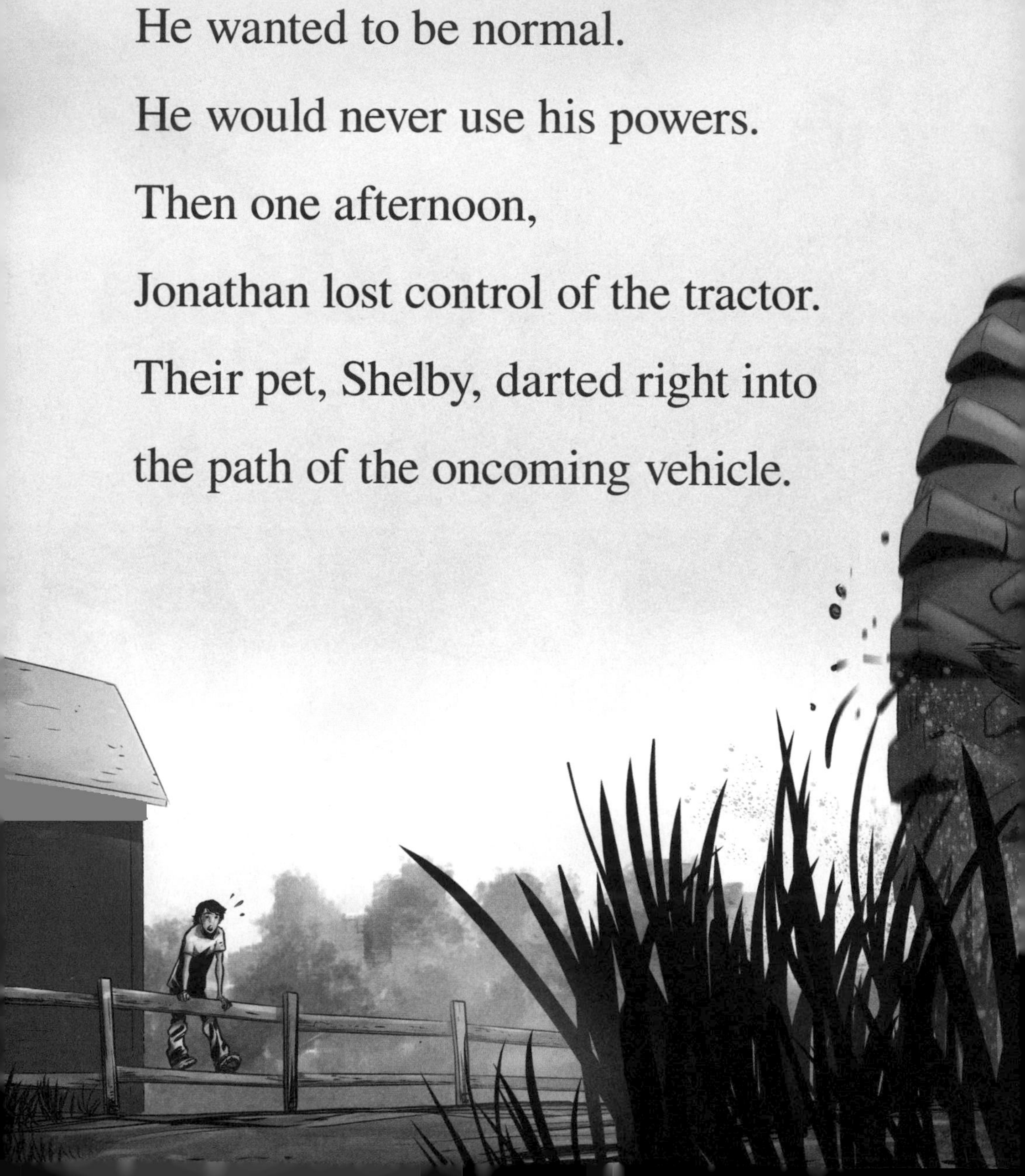

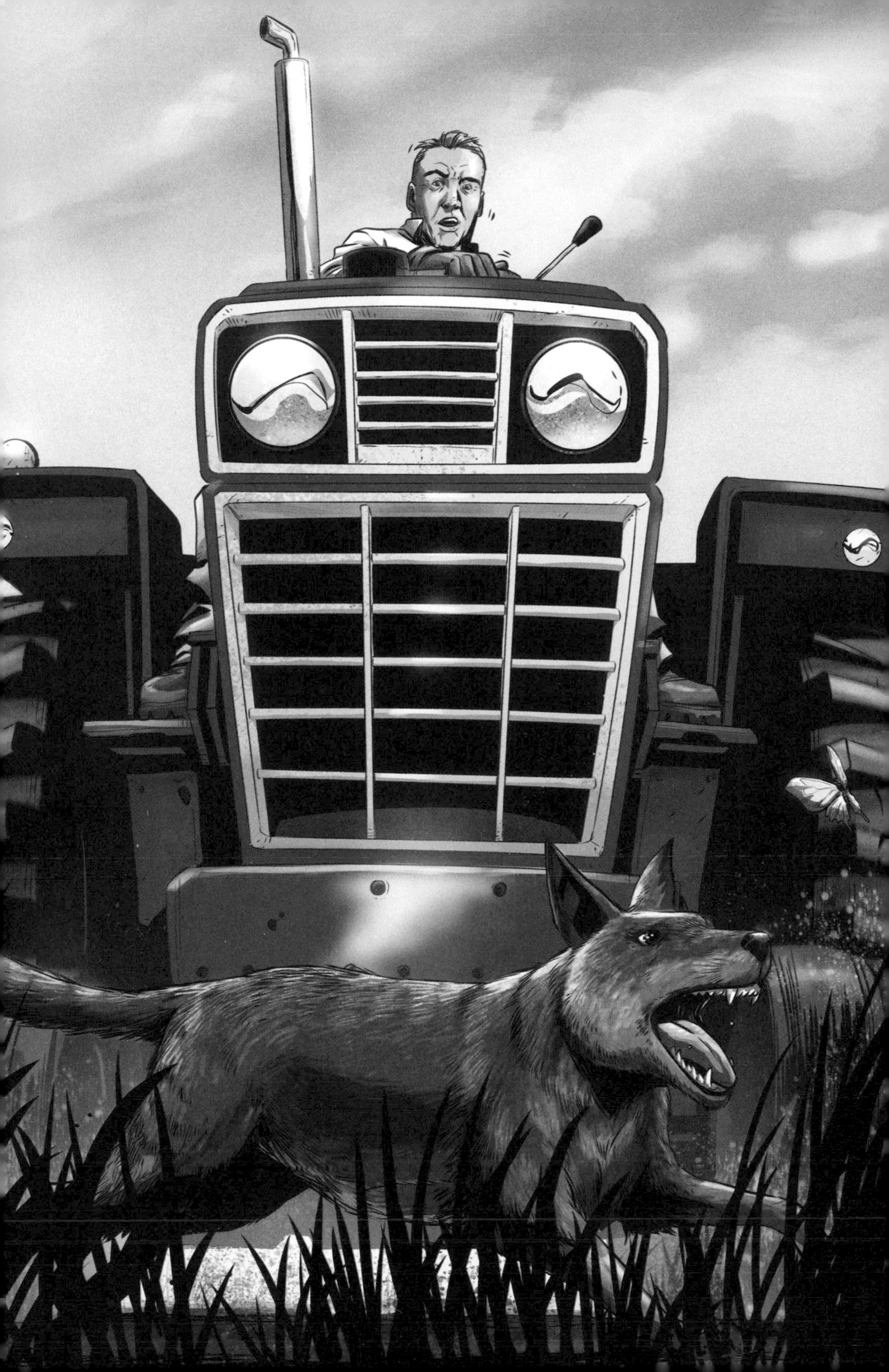

Clark used his super-speed

and rushed to the rescue.

He scooped up Shelby,

bringing the dog to safety.

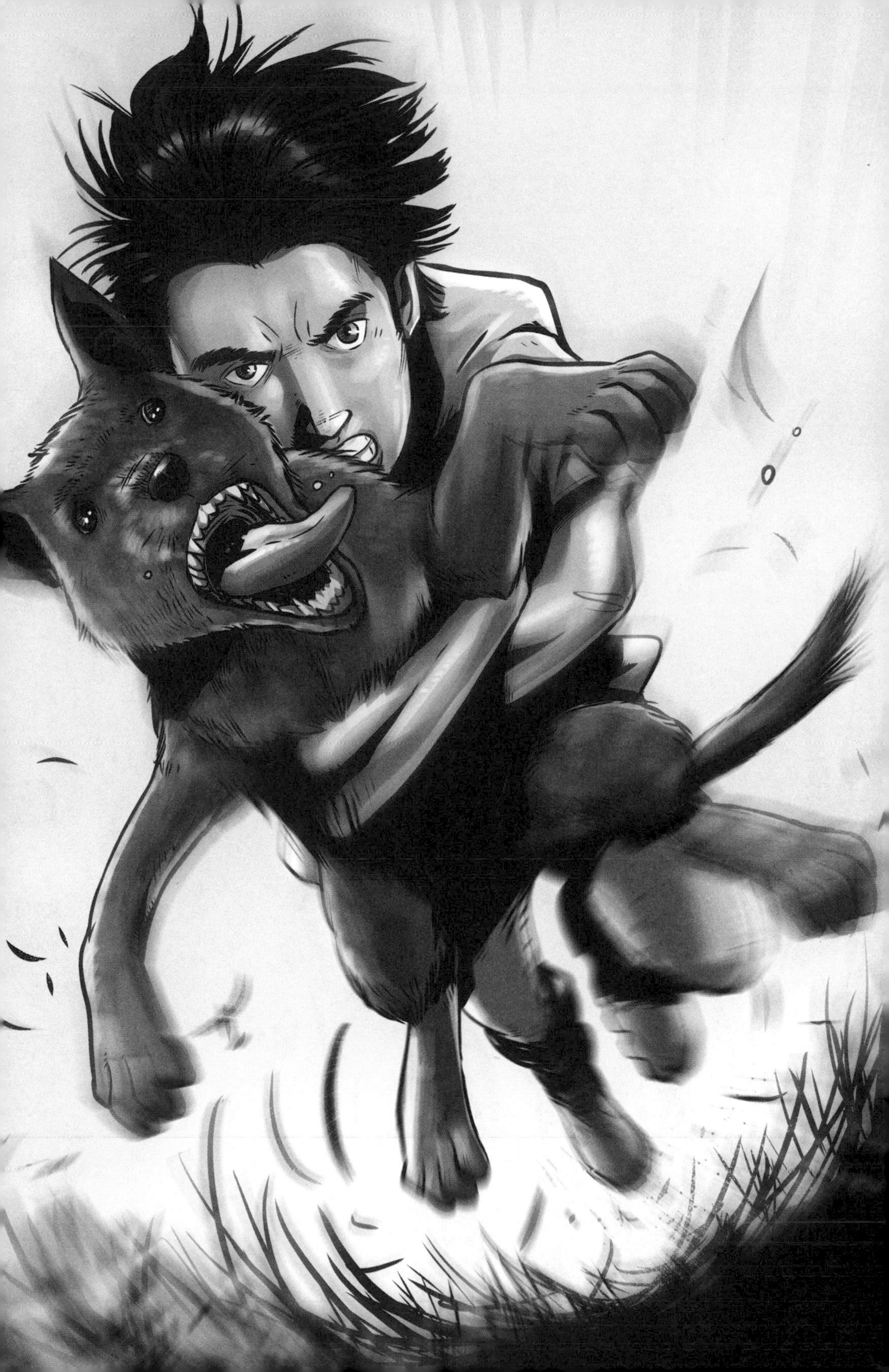

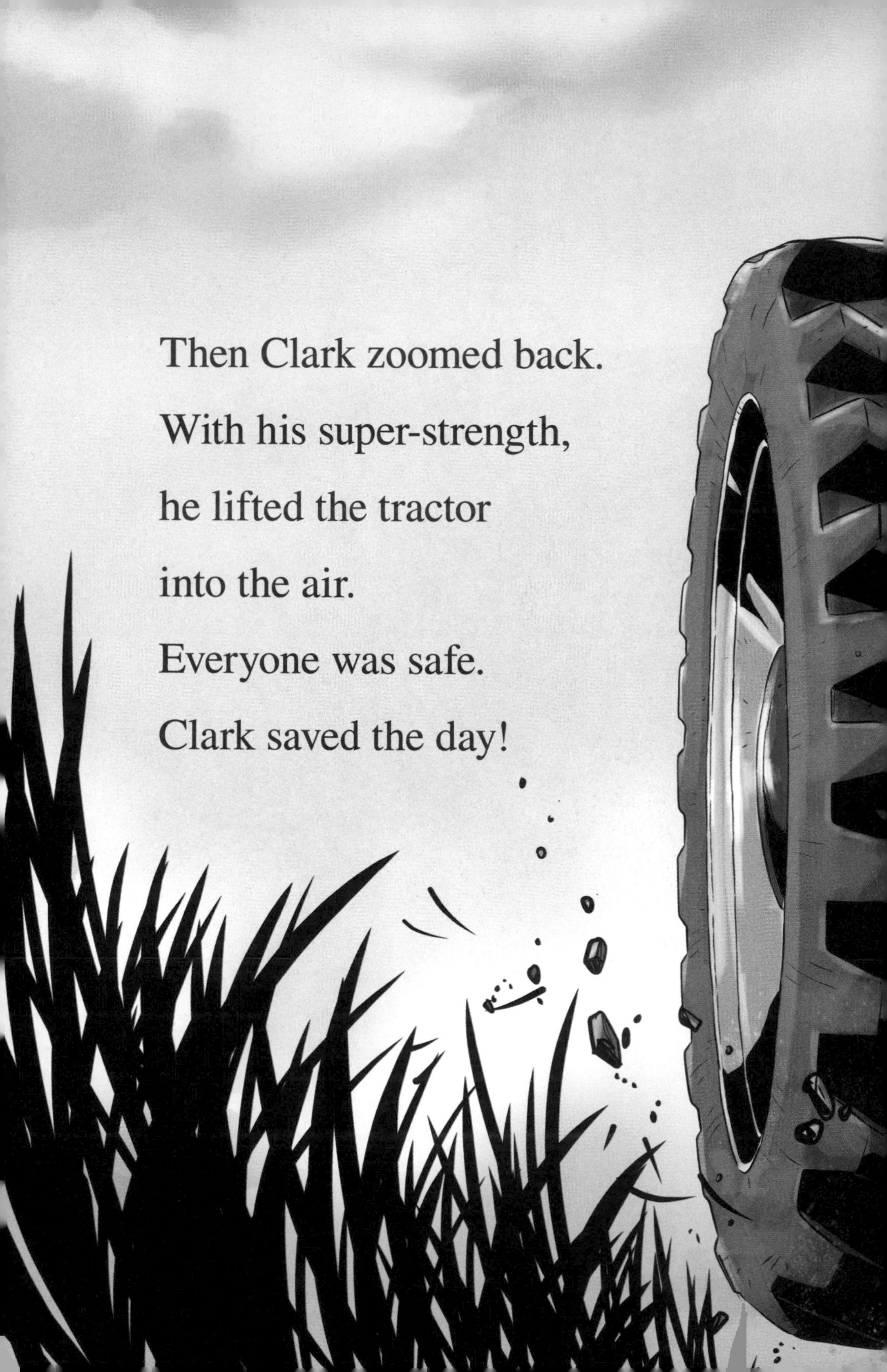

Then Clark zoomed back.
With his super-strength,
he lifted the tractor
into the air.
Everyone was safe.
Clark saved the day!

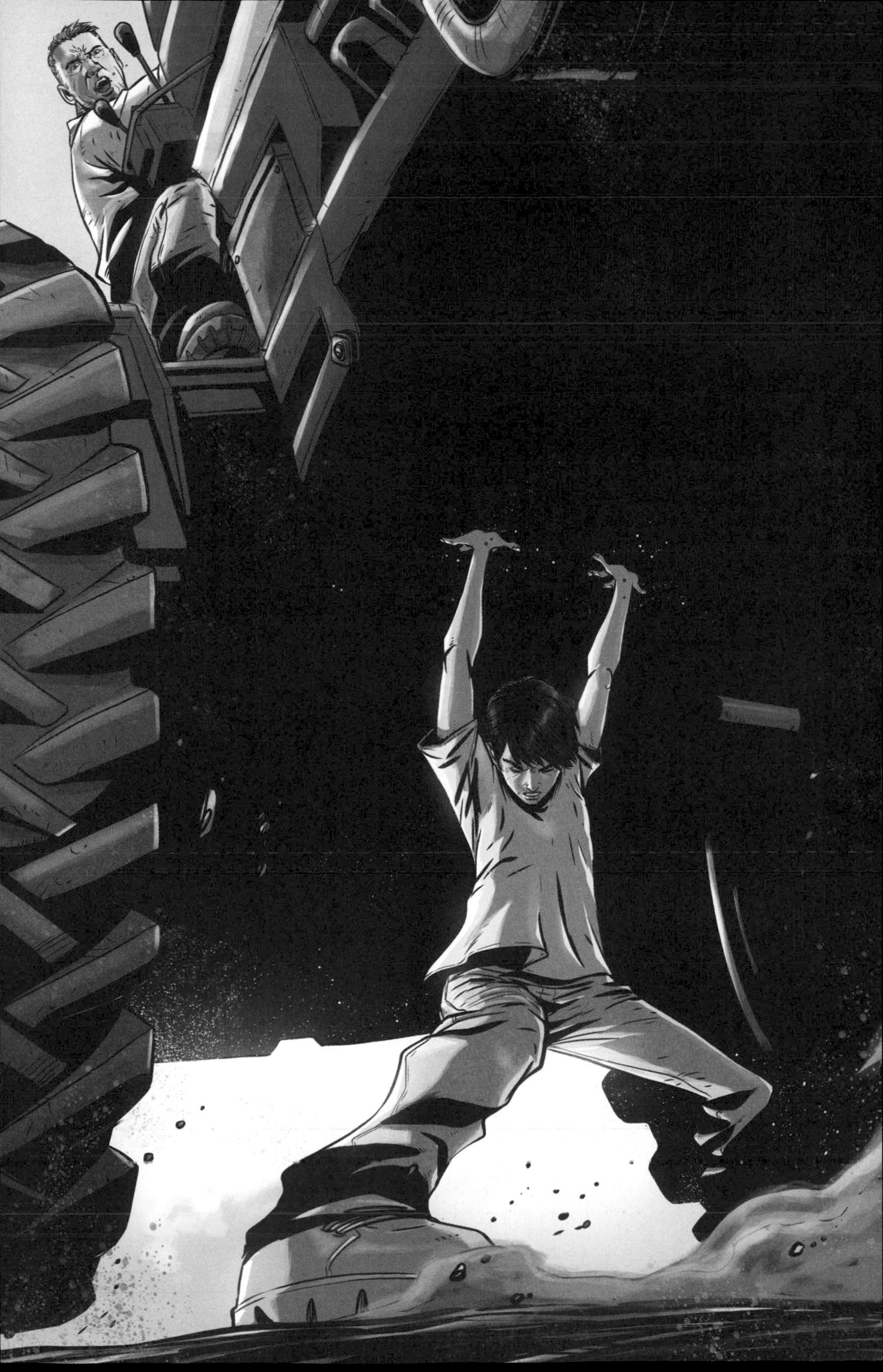

Clark knew that he had made

the wrong choice before.

He could not run away

from who he was.

When he grew up,

he traveled the globe

to help people in danger.

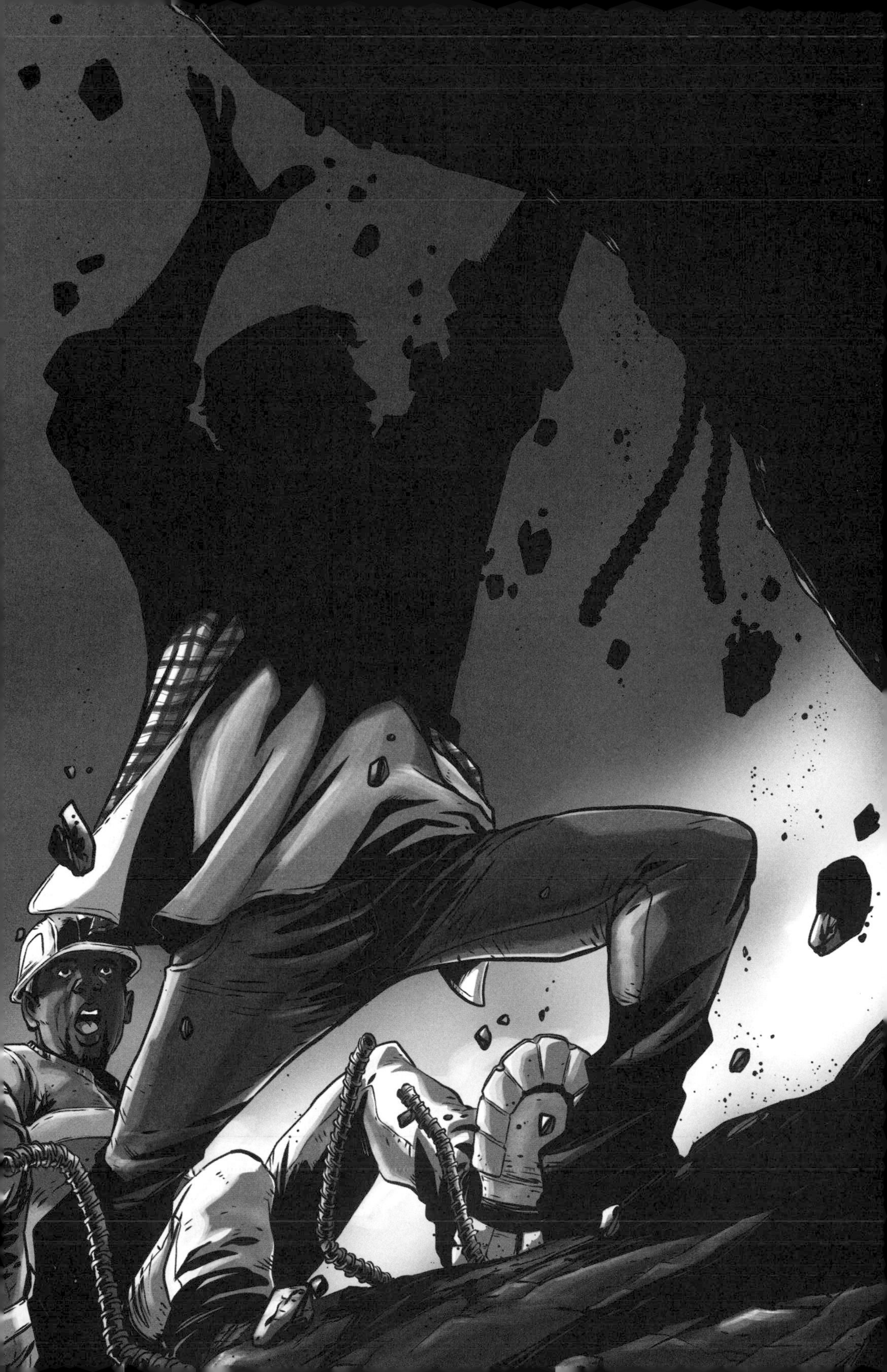

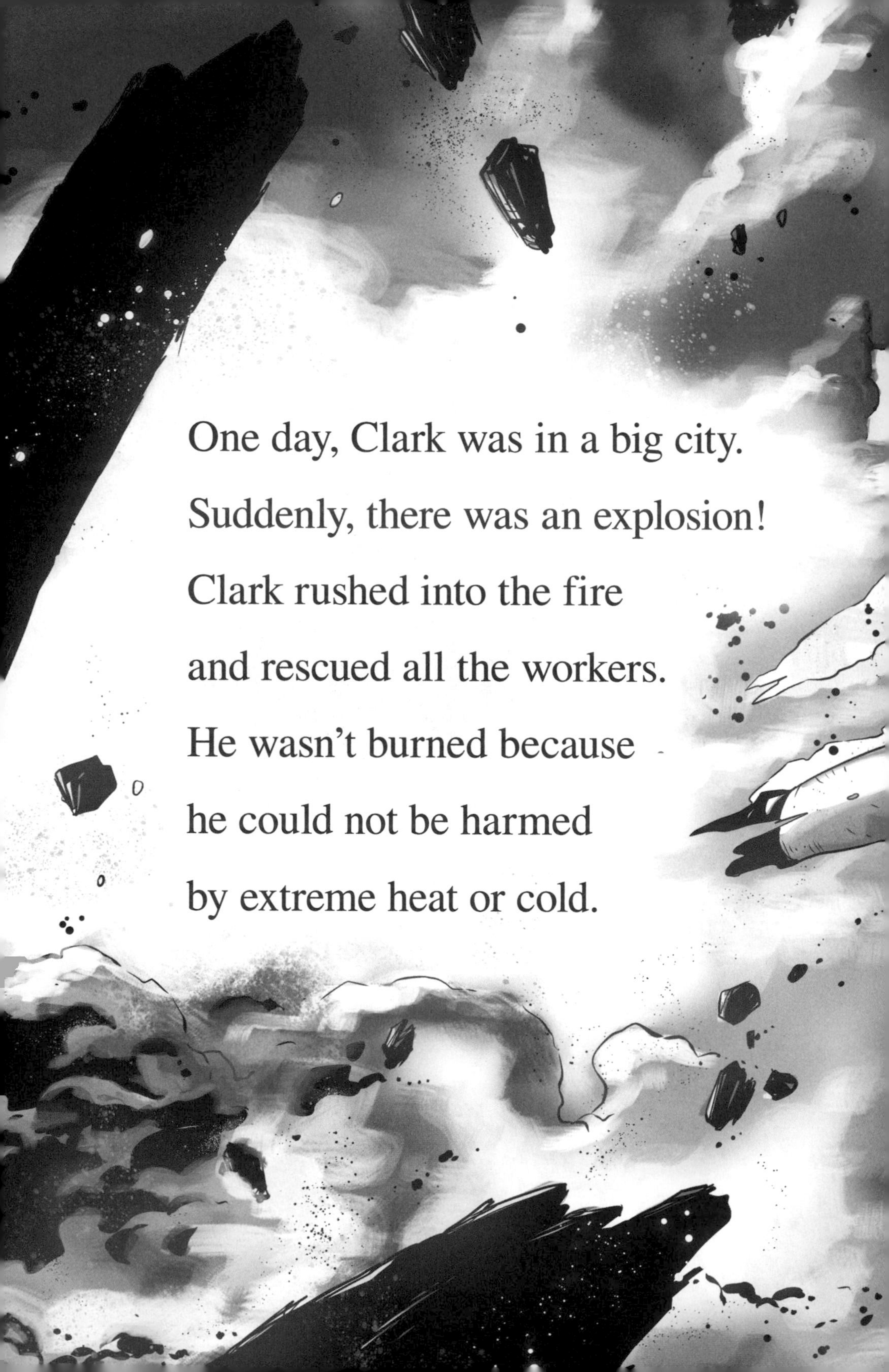

One day, Clark was in a big city.
Suddenly, there was an explosion!
Clark rushed into the fire
and rescued all the workers.
He wasn't burned because
he could not be harmed
by extreme heat or cold.

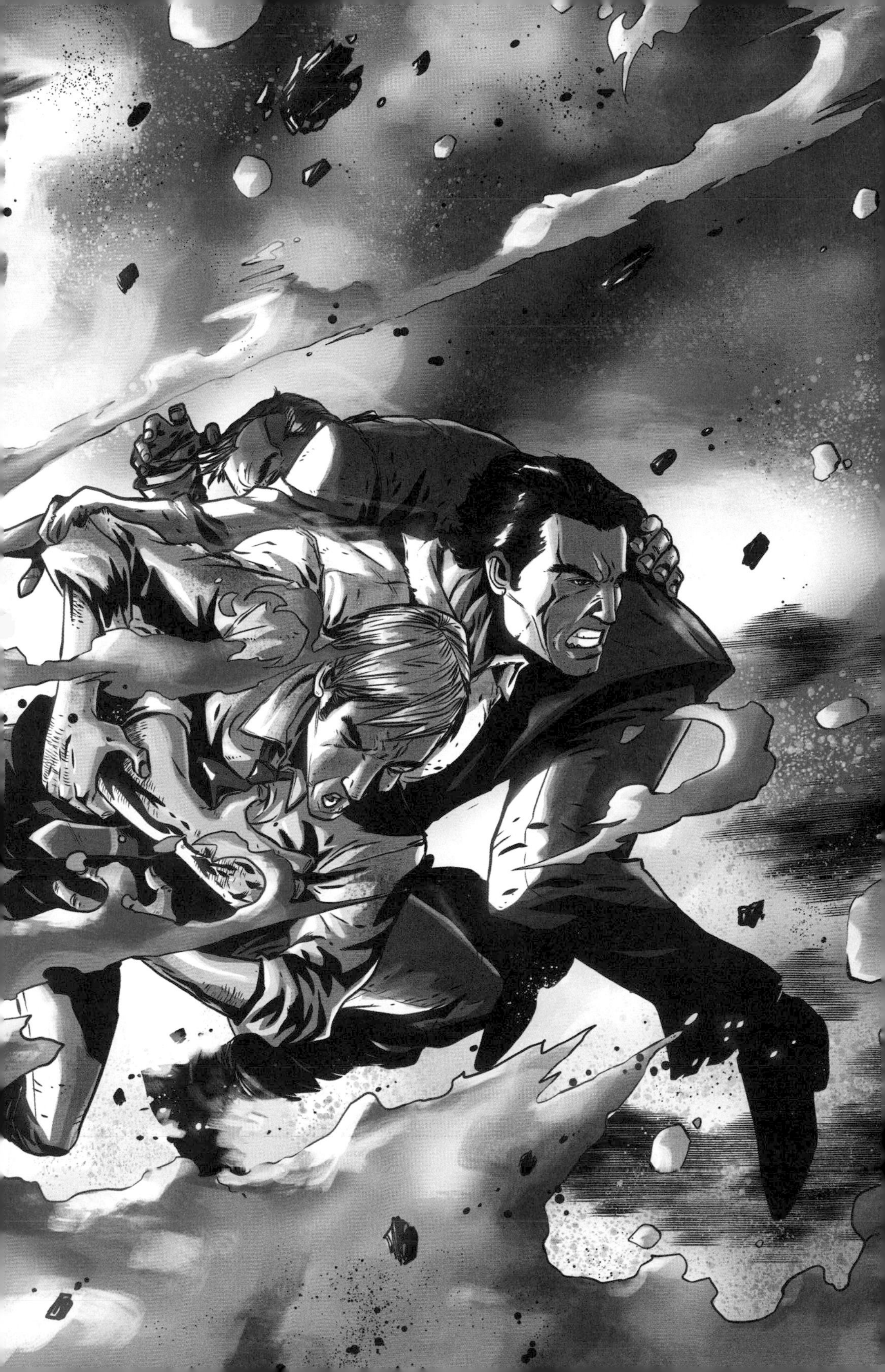

The newspapers wrote stories
about this mystery hero.
One gave him a special name—
Superman!
He was now a symbol of hope.
Clark accepted his new role
and put on a special suit to go with it.

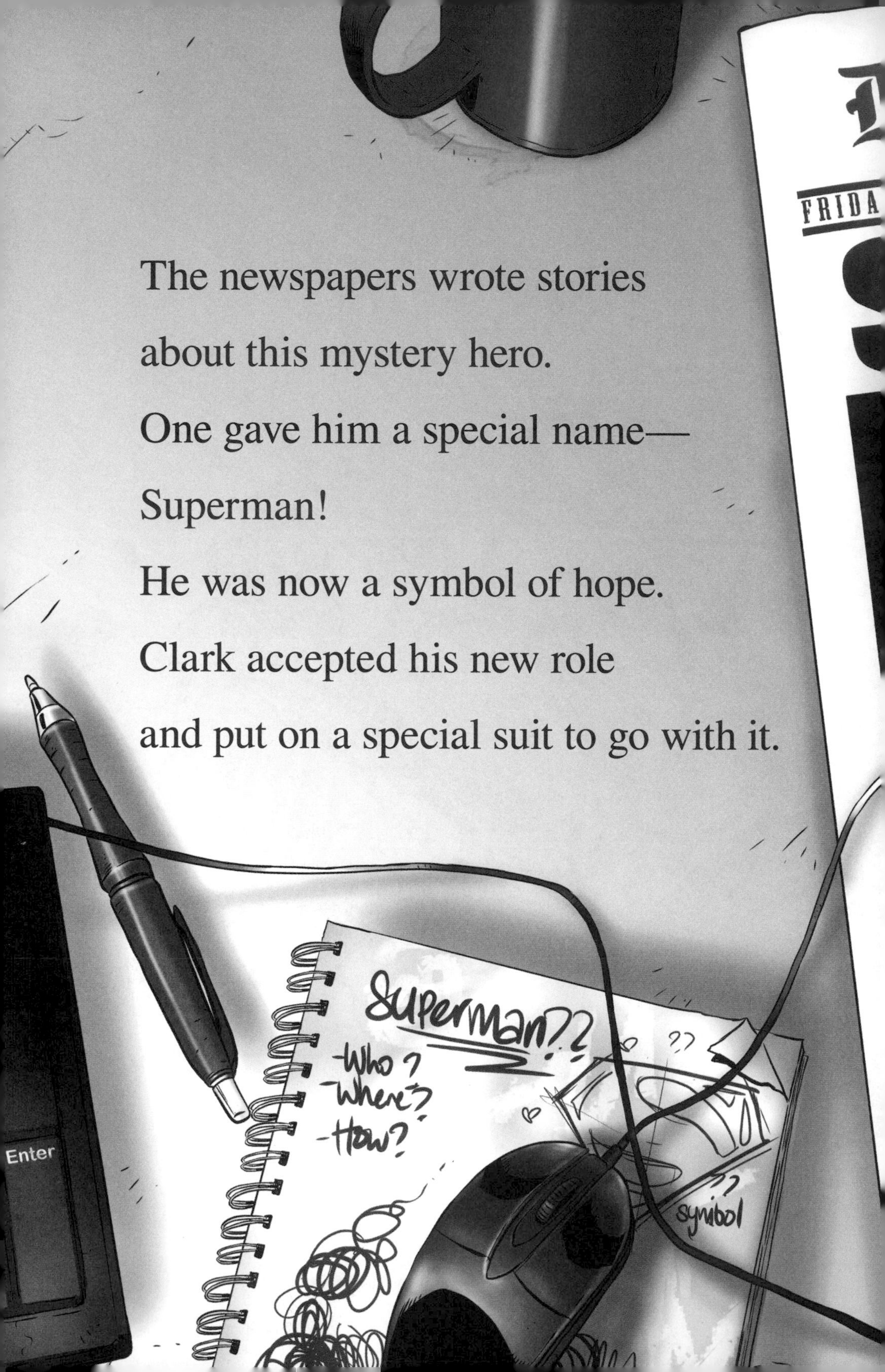
Superman??
-Who?
-Where?
-How?
??
symbol
Enter

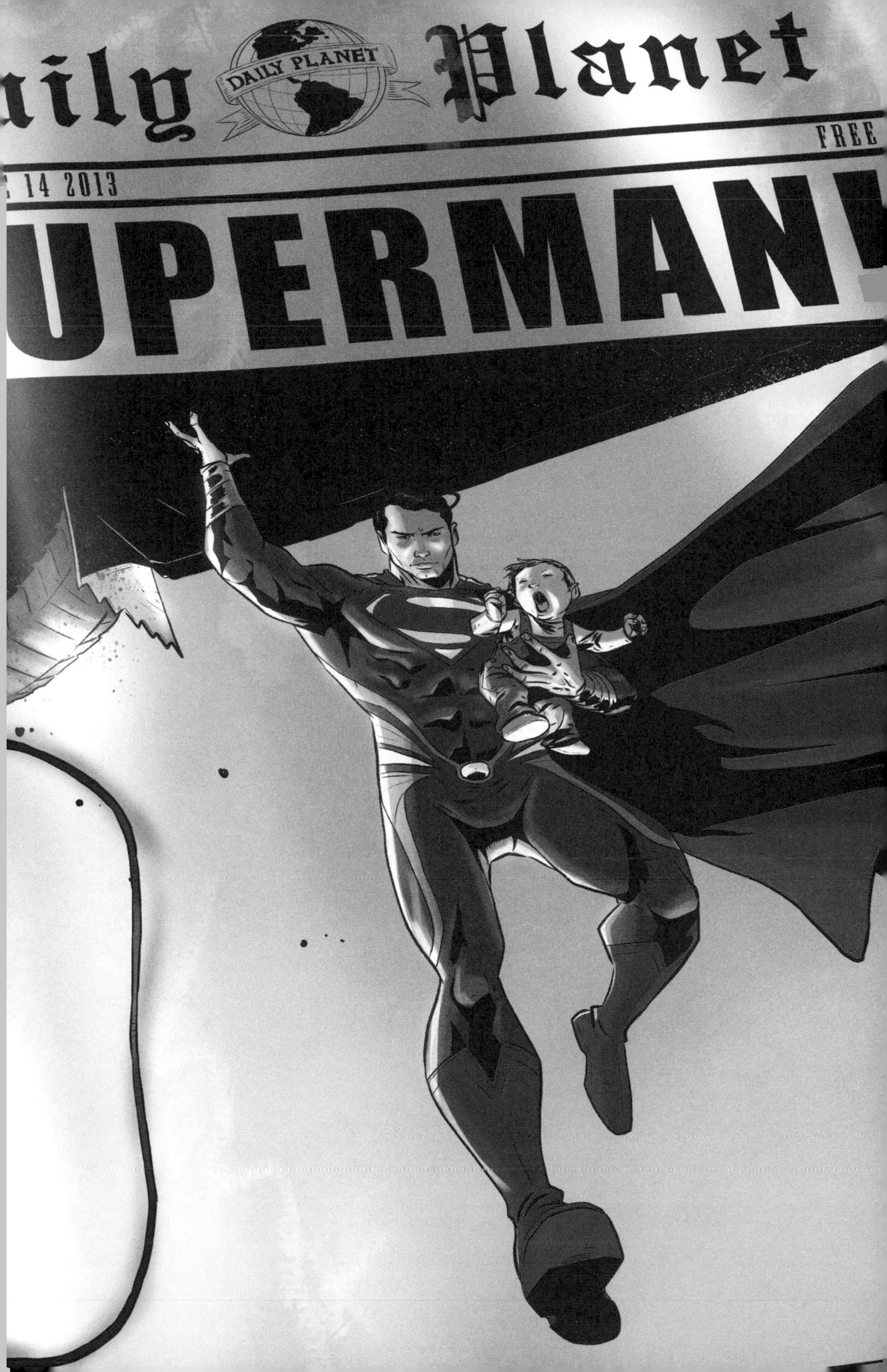

aily Planet
DAILY PLANET
FREE
14 2013
UPERMAN

Now Clark proudly uses his powers
to help keep the world safe.

He is Superman—the Man of Steel!

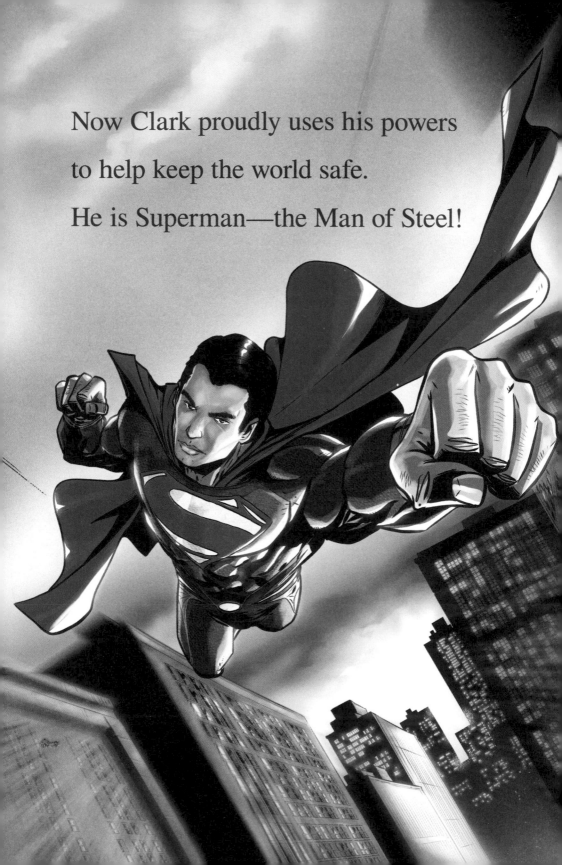